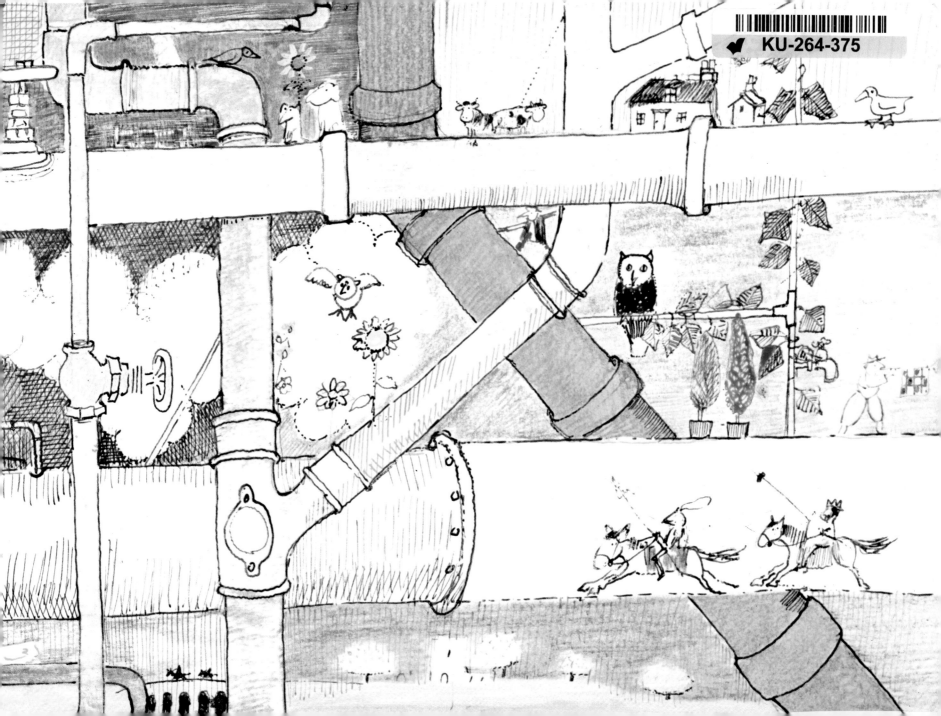

Time to

irley

Time to get out of the bath, Shirley

John Burningham

Red Fox

by the same author

CANNONBALL SIMP
BORKA
TRUBLOFF
ABC
MR GUMPY'S OUTING
AROUND THE WORLD IN EIGHTY DAYS
MR GUMPY'S MOTOR CAR
COME AWAY FROM THE WATER, SHIRLEY
SEASONS
WOULD YOU RATHER . . .
THE SHOPPING BASKET
AVOCADO BABY
GRANPA
WHERE'S JULIUS?
JOHN PATRICK NORMAN MCHENNESSY – THE BOY WHO WAS ALWAYS LATE
ALDO
HARQUIN – THE FOX WHO WENT DOWN THE VALLEY
OI! GET OFF OUR TRAIN

A Red Fox Book. Published by Random House Children's Books,
20 Vauxhall Bridge Road, London SW1V 2SA.

First published in 1978 by Jonathan Cape Ltd
First published in paperback by Young Lions 1985
Red Fox edition 1994

3 5 7 9 10 8 6 4 2

RANDOM HOUSE UK Limited Reg. No. 954009
ISBN 0 09 920051 1

Are you listening to me now, Shirley?

You haven't left the soap
in the bath again,
have you?

Some people don't
even have baths

Have you been using
this towel, Shirley,
or was it your father?

Look at your clothes all over the floor

This was clean on
this morning and just
look at it now

I wish you would learn
to fold up your clothes nicely

I have better things to do than run around tidying up after you

I'm just going
to get your nightie

Now there's water everywhere!

THE BIG ALFIE AND ANNIE ROSE STORYBOOK
by Shirley Hughes
OLD BEAR
by Jane Hissey
OI! GET OFF OUR TRAIN
by John Burningham
DON'T DO THAT!
by Tony Ross
NOT NOW, BERNARD
by David McKee
ALL JOIN IN
by Quentin Blake
THE WHALES' SONG
by Gary Blythe and Dyan Sheldon
JESUS' CHRISTMAS PARTY
by Nicholas Allan
THE PATCHWORK CAT
by Nicola Bayley and William Mayne
MATILDA
by Hilaire Belloc and Posy Simmonds
WILLY AND HUGH
by Anthony Browne
THE WINTER HEDGEHOG
by Ann and Reg Cartwright
A DARK, DARK TALE
by Ruth Brown
HARRY, THE DIRTY DOG
by Gene Zion and Margaret Bloy Graham
DR XARGLE'S BOOK OF EARTHLETS
by Jeanne Willis and Tony Ross
WHERE'S THE BABY?
by Pat Hutchins